# INDIAN

# GIRL

THE GIRL WITH CHARM, BRAVE AND POWER.

By

# Yasaswisrisai

## Tripuraneni

# ABOUT AUTHOR......

YASASWISRISAITRIPURANENI,YOUNGINDIANAUTHOR. SHE STARTED WRITING AT THE AGE OF 12, SHE MAKES PEOPLE TO LIVE IN REALITY BY HER WRITINGS, HER BOOKS DESCRIBES ALL THE PARTS OF LIFE AND USED TO THINK ABOUT ALL THE THINGS LIKE NATURE, SOCIETY, UNIVERSE AND OTHERS,MANY MORE INTERESTING AND INTERESTING PARTS OF LIFE, IN REALITY, TO LIVE IN REALITY, MANY MORE INTERESTING STORY'S OF REALITY, UNIVERSE, NATURE, LITERATURE, SCIENCE, PEOPLE, SOCIETY, NATION, COUNTRY AND MANY MORE.

www.amazon.com/author/yasaswisrisaitripuraneni

www.facebook.com/yasaswisrisaitripuraneni

www.twitter.com/@yasaswisrisai

www.instagram.com/yasaswisrisaitripuraneni

# EPILOGUE

**This** book is about an Indiangirl. Here it is to describe how Indian girls are and what are their desires, problems, and what they want to achieve and reality, painful journeys of Indian women, etc. In this book, all these are being discussed with the girl named Abiya. This name is not meant anyone or anymore it's just a character name. And the other names and places are not meant by anyone or anymore. If any spell mistakes or sentence mistakes please for give,Hope you could enjoy reading this fiction story.



Coverdesignby

Yasaswisrisai Tripuraneni

5

# CONTENT

# The journey begins...

Once a young man used to live in a village named kapiri. He used to work as daily labour.His name wasAnand, he is a very hardworking man who believes in hard work leads to success and that makes him one fine day a farmer from daily labour. he owned one acre of land .He earned this by saving his wages. He used to spend money only on his daily needs .As he wants to earn money he also used work under a big farmer .one fine day he found a very gorgeous girl and decided to marry and he connived this proposal to that girl and they got married. As they got married he started managing his financial crisis. He was debited a lot. He thought marriage makes him financial crisis but one day he understands marriage doesn't make that so with courage he want to start a small business and wants to be a rich man in the village but after one year they are blessed with a baby girl. They named the baby girl as Abiya. She was a very beautiful girl.

He wants to plan his daughter's future but due to his financial crisis. He can't effort her to study and village people teased him because he want to send abiya to school and they used to treat girls as there is no use of sending girls to school if we send them to school they may fight with us and they may be higher in family and society and they believed girls for kitchen only so they are not allowed to get educated , he used to take her to field and work along with him in the field. That year due to lack of rainfall he doesn't grow crop much and he has debited again and the big farmer asked him to pay the total money within two days but he couldn't pay the money and finally, the big farmer has taken along with him the little six years baby girl to work as a maid in his home but the baby can't do the household chores and the big farmer wasn't feeding her at least once a day but she doesn't want to work but she want to go school. And she was torched like she was teased by farmer's wife and they used to treat them very bad as they are lower caste people and they are not allowed to sit at their home and couldn't allowed to drink water or tohave some food or look at them and poor girls are used to treat as they can't do any thing and they are only for look up family and children's needs ,Abiya was beaten by sharp cane. She became very thin andlean and she is suffering from high fever and cold but her parents can't help her they are effortless and if abiya ask the big farmer to give a hand full of rice then he used to remove her clothes and romed around the house and beating with hard cane but he couldn't give rice.And dailybig farmer used to beat abiya with hard and sharpen rope .The little baby girl couldn't bare the pain she is about to die if the big farmer continues like this

Every day beating and teasing her and she was bleeding but she want to live and enjoy with friends and with her parent's.parents came to know about this but they can't question him if they questioned big farmer he will kill them and her parents can't help her they are effortless and there is the only option to them is to pay back the money and after knowing about abiya some people in the village felt very sad and some  said leave her she will die in big farmer hand then their will be no problem and your money willsavewithoutspendingf or her.but day by day abiya was loosing her strength and was bleeding more but she want to fullfill her wishes so she want to fight with big farmer for her rights and big farmer was planning her to sell for some one if their parent's could not pay the total money.Abiya came to know about this she thought only to fight with big farmer or escape after selling to some one.at last big farmer again torcherd her at that time abiya thought to fight with big farmer she came to fight but suddenly she remembered her parents so she keept calm and she beared the pain again. After two days big farmer sold abiya to someone then at that time of selling her she thought to escapewhile travelling .she was travelling in the forest in mean while found some rocks she collected those rocks and she built a statue of her and she covered with some clothes which she is having with her.she escaped from that person and went near her parents then her parents felt very sad after looking at her . Then that night after sleeping of villagers he took abiya to a cave and left her their and given some food and he returned to home. The next morning After that the person came to check abiya in big farmer house and in village but he couldn't find her  finally their parents paid the debt after two years. In mean while her father used to go to that cave and look after abiya.they asked big farmer to return their child but he said he don't know about the child.After three weeks abiya returned to home.At that moment they decided to send Abiya to school and wants Abiya to get educated and Abiya is very much interested and wants becoming high in her life. And started studying. At beginning she faced many insults from villagers but she felt very sad about it she felt no one support girls to get educated and she thought not to listen to their words and not to stop going to school because she was remembered the pain and how she was torcherd by the big farmer at first she was not allowed to sit in class she used to sit out side of the class and listen to class and the teacher didn't took care of her that was the first  a girl entering into school to get educated and some rich girls are used to  tease her and used to stole her books and tear those books and fire those books but abiya felt very sad she  felt atleast even a girl is not helping or encouraging another girl to get out from this evil and she faced many insults one day she thought that if we fight with insults their will not be more insults and she started fighting with those insults then every one in the village and other people who used to tease her and insult her they shut uped their mouths.After few days she saw how her parents are efforting to send her to school so she went to field in  the morning and to school in night while she is going to school big farmer used to stop her and used to scold her but she didn't care so one day big  farmer  send  some people to stop her going to school.then while she is going they caught her and  beat  her  but  she bravely  escaped  from them  she  thrown  red chilli  powder  into  their eyes and she beat them with the same hard cane and she ran away  from them.one fine night she completed her midnight school and returning to home at the time a man asked her to take chocolate and she took the chocolate and run away from him.But the man also runs along with her to catch her and  she was caught by him and he tanned away with her to a dark place where anyone could not find him,her and the place is very scary ,filled with blood of humans and animals are moving from one cadaver to next cadaver and having flesh and blood of humans as drink then she woke up saw the place she was very scary first but she wants to live and wants to see her parents happy .so she decided to escape from the place she kept on moving from one area to another and then he found the girl was missing. He started checking out her in the dark area but he couldn't discover her and he didn't had dare to enter to all the area's of the world. she found out an amazing world as she keeps moving she found a world full of chocolate and funny people and next she also discovered a world with demons and their does demons caught abiya and taught to kill her but abiya bravely escaped from them.But those demons searched for her and they found her and started killing her. But they dissaper but she could hear those demons voice and she taught to kill them so she found some people are dancing and singing and others are crying and some are going to die, the other's are enjoying she also found that some beautiful nature and some are enjoying the new relations withother's and their she found a little magicworld with lot of amazing wonder's she was searching to get out of the dark place. Then she found the last area of that world there on the wall it was written that

"what all you have know is created and given to you it may be life and every thing ,is every thing permanent and why do striving for everything and loosing one thing doesn't make you happy and right just live your own destiny of that your real life wants than to live other's life" and she found a place to escape from that world while she is leaving she found a piece of paper and the words that written on it is "leave out the  great fear in you and come out with the thrown in you by the dare" later she remembered those words but she was finding the real meaning of those words.And her parents are very upset about her missing. She was missing for a week. And ultimately she found out that area where she could escape from the tragic place. She found a trench where she could reach out to big farmer's house. She started going to that cave. In middle of the cave She could found one golden box she tried to open it but she doesn't opened it ,came out of that cave andshe a found place. She found a trench where she could reach out to  big farmer's house. She startup going to that canal. She could found one gold box she tried to open it but she doesn't opened it ,she a found a old palace ,the palace is full of human's body's so she decided to keep it there and moved on and finally she reached her family. Her parents are very much happy. and after she reached her home.after few weeks one scholar heard about this and she was gifted a pen and a book by him. she felt very glad. Then she decided to become an educated girl.

This makes her study and works hard and her father

decided to send her only school, not for farmstead.

# ThelittleAbiyagoes to school…

The little Abiya was welcomed to enter into the school ,she is very happy and pleased. She is very much eager to study more and wants to grow high in life. She believes that hard work with interest leads to success in life. Early days she could not understand what they teach. Yet she found some friends and at the beginning, they used to help her to understand what the teacher teaches. She used to enjoy with her friends .she made some friends named Raju, Neha, Amish, varuvan, Mira. They used to play under a neem barrier. They used to make toys with clay and mud they enjoy a lot and used to dance in the rain and all together would have lunch under a mango tree. Their school is surrounded by greenery plants and some creatures. They used to live happily and all together used to take a bath under beautiful waterfalls. She lived happily one fine day Varuvan, Raju didn't come to school and went out into the forest

Then they found the Hazard snake and they Grabbed the snake and

bought to the head Master table. After the

The headmaster sat on

The chair he looked at the hazard the snake he was very scary and ran Away both the boys laughed and enjoy a lot.

Later Neha and Abiya came to know about this

And scolded them but the naughty boys enjoyed the fun and they both use to sleep in class and makes a lot of fun in the class they may do it just for fun but all the teachers are haterd by them and they used to write exams very well and score high marks but Neha and Abiya used to score the average but all these are always very close to each other. One fine day all the friends went to the lake for a bath and they had a bath and dance on the hard rocks and they found an elephant all the boys and girls jump from the tree on an elephant and elephant and the boys, girls had a cool shower under the waterfall they enjoyed a lot and returned to the home. All the people are happy and they used to go to school and learn daily and they are very happy and after one year all the must go to high school for high school. As Neha father was very rich she went to Delhi for her higher studies and Abiya went to the next village for her higher studies and Raju is a very poor boy so he could remain in the same village and used to help his parents and varuvan went to Mumbai for his higher studies so all the friends are going dipus and they sad and all the friends before dipus they meet at waterfalls all the friends are very sad but they decided to meet at the same after ten years

# Abiya enters to vipirini.......

Abiya's family has to move to the next village name vipirini. They live happily and **Abiya** joined in high school. Their she couldn't find any good friends she is very upset and she missed her childhood best friends and all the other classmates in the high school would not support her and anyone wouldn't like to talk with her and teachers also used to discourage her she is very upset and one fine day a rich man in the village wants to get Abiya to his home because she is very much talented and intelligent so he takes to his home offer to have lunch at his house but the rich man wife is bad women she likes only rich people but not poor people and she could not serve food for her but the rich man served the food and he takes care of his education and Abiya's father used to work under this rich man as a farmer and she used to tease by his classmates in high school so she was very upset and wants to show them that she is a courageous girl so she started working very hard but she used to fail in exams .she failed the first exam but she was very upset and decided to work hard than before but she failed many times but she used to try all the times so one day she sat alone under a tree and she starts thinking and she starts realizing what she Is .as she started thinking of it she aroused many questions and she started finding answers for her questions and she understands and she realized everyone on this earth is not perfect in every part in this world and she decided that we should take the moment and we should make it perfect. And no need to be perfect in all the parts

Just to be real and she keept moving .she was rejected and scolded by her teachers and she is abused by her high school friends and classmates And also by the village people because she is not rich and she decided to keep move and trying to reach the high peaks of the life this all made her mentally strong so she could face every hard situation with the courage.Then one fine day while she was going to school some boys teased her and daily they teased her but she didn't noticed them then one of them thought to kidnapped abiya one fine day they kidnapped abiya and they thought to have some physical attack on her first they striped with blade on her body and some other boys thought have sex with her but at that time those boys went out so abiya heared about this and thinking to escape from those evil. Without making noise first she removed the ropes tied to her hands and without making nosie she jumped from the wall and she ranned away to her house her mother asked what happened? But she replied nothing then that night she was very upset and she was very much terrified to say this to her parents or even parents and she decided to compliant about this in school. So the next day she sai this what happened to her to head master of the school. Then head master called those boys and suspened from school for five years and they punished                    ,their punishment is to work as workers and help every women in the village for five years.so other student understand that without terrifying we should fight with those evil and complian to elder's .if They don't complian for their family pride or name fame then how to get justified for good and to be punished by evil .other girls inspired by abiya and they got confidence to fight and by seeing her many girls in the village came forward with those evil and they complained bravely to headmaster how they are abused by some boys and teachers also.after this those boys are very anger on  abiya they planned to kill her. They plaaned to kill her at night after every one are slepping they went abiya house to kill but they heard these words that 'A girl is giving birth to boys and girls but why she is treated as she is the only for family needs and others physical works why boys don't think that every girl is her sister and women are their mother .so by listening to these words they went away from abiya house and they felt very sad for what they did for abiya and they changed their behaviour and started helping women and used to treat every girl as their sister and women as their mother.After that she concentrated more on her studies So she tried very hard and finally succeeded and she was very happy. And her parents and everyone is happy and everyone in the village used to praise the Anand and Abiya and Anand before he dreamt to start up a small business and he was trying to plan it and Abiya was trying to go to the city for study and her family decided not to move to the city and she is only going to study alone in the city and she is so sad and she doesn't know how to move in the city and she doesn't know how to cook and other basic things and they don't have relatives in the city.so one day she went near her mom named Rumika.

# The Realwords from mom...

Then Abiya asked her mom about how to live in the city and how to move among people and how girls move with men and elders, boys. Her mother had replied that in her childhood days girls are not allowed for education and then entering into the temple, girls used to marry in their childhood and they are only for household chores and other like getting married and no education and take care of husband's family and other issues in those days there is no freedom girl child, and if the husband dies girl also should die along with him, they used to treat her like a slave work without wages but in ancient days women are treated like a goddess like Lakshmi, Saraswati, Durga in India according to ancient Hindustan. For example, in olden days Draupadi, wife of five Pandavas was, used by them on the dice like goods and women were also used for dance and to please the kings in ancient days and women are not allowed to speak loudly with men and they can't question the works of the men and even they are not allowed to participate in social and economics, politics, and personal activities.and after many leaders fought for the freedom of the girl's education and the first women king in India was rani Rudrama Devi and Jhansi Lakshmi Bhai is the great warrior who fought with British later women empowerment get started and present women are in every part but we can't say that every woman is not part of this even today some women are can't get even basic education but some parts women have the freedom and some women are misusing it and they become evil to the society and in historical times the women enjoyed a comparatively very high status during Vedic period. In other parts of the world, women are being a productive member of society .the conditions of the Vedic women was very good and women enjoyed the religious status. The high social status of the women of those days. but the status of the women they are not treated equally with the men. Though the women participated in the family ceremony they only played the role of the silent observer, not an active participant. As per Manu, even men have always enjoyed the unchallenged authority over their wives. child marriages, polygamy, and sati prevalent at that time still out of these things women are respected in the society.supports of bhakti movements were expounded and spoken about equality of women with men. they not free even to go elsewhere without husband's permission.but in Vedic period position of women was not worse as that of today. That woman in the

Vedic period was also strong footage as compared to men. During those days men were polygamy and widow burning was an accepted norm. Though the overall position of women was lower than Men, yet, on the whole, the positions of women were not so good, women started being discriminated against on the ground of education and other parts and the Child marriage. And physical chastity of women and they are unquestioned obedience to husband leads to progressive deterioration of their position. The strongest woman being honored. The women who don't obey their heads of the family or the husband they are torched by the and in those days who are very strong and enough to fight with men are very few great women's later the times and everything changes by that time women got little freedom to get out of the home. before they are being torched by the men after the great social movements by the socialist women got the freedom to step into this world .this movements many rejections and oppositions, many women are died and torched and the men who support them would treat them like the one who can't achieve anything and they also get abused and teased by the society and even today some parts of the world same situations going on and they being punished in some kings used to kill if arise their word against to them and some kings who support them and would encourage them .and in ancient days women would have an unhappy married life. As by passage of the times, the positions of the women became worse. Like only high caste used to get the education, they use to get education separated from boys. they don't have the freedom that they cant choose their goals they are assisted to follow the elders .later the women status in the society they are privileged that they had widow remarried and stop sati sagamanam. they are not allowed inter-caste marriages . and so many other issues.And in those a widow women is not supposed to remarry and if any one remarried they used feel very bad for family pride in the society and some women in the family they torchered for more dowry and some are abused and torcherd by husbands and some they torched by mother-in-law and some are being torched by sister-in-law and by brother-in -law they are blackmailed and they are forced to have some sex or money and many more or they are abused in the family and and spoil her own name in the family and in some areas a women who went out for some needs with other men thay used to think they had some relation ship and other matters and some women who goes for work they are abusedand they teased but they can't complian what happened to them because they are afraid of family or some higher's and their own name or something but without complaining against to evil how to change this evil and cruel world and some are facing harresement by neighbour's or even more in social media they are being teased and harresed by their photos or videos and even some others and blackmails and many more for all this cruel people only one thing is the solution is not to fear for those evil and thinking about other issues like family or some thing they need to stand up by their own amd fight with it.laterwomen's empowerment was started . All these are explained to abiya by her mother before she goes to the city and then she understands how women faced hard situations so she decided to be a very bravery girl. Then she decided to fight against evil people. And with her father's help, she decided to go to the city and join the college. Then before she goes to the city she learned how to cook and other household chores.

with her father support, she applied for st.francis college and the is accepted to join.

# ST.FRANCIS WELCOMED ABIYA.........

Anand joined abiya in the st Francis and she used to stay in girls hostel. She used to go  college daily one day she found a man lying on the footpath then with the help of her neighbor and friend she took him to hospital. she used to go to college and returned to the hostel.

One fine day she meets men and that man promised her to take to purchase books and other necessary accessories then she believed him and went along him. But he cheated the girl and robbed money from her. Then she understands that not to believe anyone and have hope on anyone. She called her father to come to twice in the month for purchasing the goods and other accessories and then she understands how her father suffers then she tries to stand up on her own and then decided to have an independent life. And she starts scurrying . and had many struggles .to earn some money she started working part-time jobs and other small kinds of jobs and at the first, she started being teased by the rowdy boys and other but she doesn't care, anyone. She understands what she can do and doesn't what other people say but she used to understand what the elders say and some she would follow. there in the college, she found very good friends and she worked hard and she understands that we should not study hard but we need to work hard.Then one fine day she meet a boy in social media then she fallen in love with that boy and later she shared her photos and sometimes they used to meet and talk for hours but after few months she understood the reality that he prposed her to have sex there is no love later he black mailed so she complained to police but they not responded correctly so she meet high officer in police he helped her.Later she concentrated   And she completed her +1 and

+2 graduation. And then need to choose her career and then she decided to do want she love not the others .she decided to see her parents happy with luxury. and then she decided to do the best in science and technology. And then she applied for it she had applied for the entrance exam but she was not qualified.

# Kidnapped......

One fine day abiya was kidnapped by rowdy's .her father and mother are very scary about this news . they informed to police and police are searching for her  then abiya was kidnapped and taken her to a dark place where any dody couldn't find her and them and they left abiya and away .she don't know where she is and they give some drugs to her so sleept for one week after one week she woke up and she saw the place she felt very scary she don't know why they kidnapped her in between police are searching for her but they didn't find her .her parents felt very sad and they don't know who has done this to them and after one week she woke up and she thought she was kidnapped by that cheater but he didn't kidnapped he relized his mistake she was kidnapped by some rowdy's later she came to know this .first she thought to escape from them but she thought to fight with but she didn't had that much energy to

fight with them    mean
while  is being torched by
the rowdy.she is torched
like they removed her nail
tips and beat with  hard
ropes    then    she    was
bleeding and they used to
beat her with   she was
trying to escape from the
rowdy, she was tied to the
chair and the rowdy went
out  for  their meal they
not given water for abiya
they thought to rape abiya

at that she fighted with them at that police had arrived to check the place and she escaped and started to running then those boys who teased abiya in vipirini they saw her and they protected abiya later they reported to police  abiya and police arrested them and reached her home safely. Her parents are happy and the rowdy was arrested by the police.

# ABIYA GOES TO UNIVERSITY...

Abiya felt very depressed about this and would stay at home for a few months and she prepared for her entrance examination coming out of the depression with help of her mother. And then she decided not to go to any kind of depression next time remembered what her mother said that how women fought against evil and she started preparing for her higher education now she aims to get an entrance to university.she understand that when we stop trying why to think about succeeding in life .she decided not to stop trying whether we may fail or win but if we fail we have learned what we have done the mistake and that mistakes make us perfect. If we win we should not pride of success and think about the most talented than you and she decided not to compare with anyone in any other aspects also because she understands everyone is unique and have their own power to succeed she understand failure makes success and she learned many great lessons in her life so she decided to first to fail in all aspects then that makes them to success .that is how we rebounce back. With that spirit, she appealed to entrance exam she worked hard and succeded in the entrance examination. she felt very had this time her mother used to come to stay with her in the city so this time she is very happy to go and study and she joined the university and started off having a new and safe environment.

She and her mother used to live happy in the city and they both used to go to movies and parks and other they are happy .with her mother support she completed her 1 st year very happy and then she decided to stay alone without anyone support and her mother returned to the home.

# Second-year of university...

Then started to live alone in a single bedroom flat then abiya meet some more new friends all the friends are very good and they used to help her, and once abiya got very sick and all her friends helped her to take her to hospital and they cared her very much. then one day she decided to help poor child girls to get the education then she decided to save her money few and help some poor child. she felt very happy about that helping child and that made her happy and felt very good so she decided to start an organization when she settled and she completed her 2 nd year without any default. one fine day she was remembering her childhood friends. She missed them a lot, after completion of her 2 nd year education she went to her village.. their she enjoyed her holidays and come back to college for 3 rd year education

# ABIYA

# FALL

# IN

# LOVE........

Abiya comes back to the city again. Again she starts going to college. one fine day a boy named

Abhishek meets Abiya .they used to share their

feelings and used to live happily together. One day he said how he comes out of the poor and started earning. Both of them shared their feelings and both of the feelings are the same she felt very happy to be with him . and the same was felt by Abhishek. And both of them went out to the park then she found the rowdy who kidnapped her she also shared that moment with him . he understands her very well. One fine day he said that he wants to live with her and she said that she felt the same and both of them are being blessed by the elders, she conveyed this one to her mother and father that both of them want to live happily and together but at the first, both of the mother and father didn't like that. but he can't leave without her but at that time she needs her mother and father and also him, by the way, to be settled and have a good future. One fine day he used to do suicide but he went to suicide but he didn't do it and the abiya feeling very sad in the inner heart and they can't one each other and her parents are deciding to marry her with some other boy then this boy came to her parents talk to her parents. then parents decided to look at this matter after completion of her education and again she returned to college and started studying very hard and work very hard, and the same boy started working very hard. they live without seeing each other

After coming to the city abiya didn't meet Abhishek. so one evening abiya went to meet Abhishek but abiya found a girl with him and she went back to her room and she cried a lot then Abhishek came with the girl and said that she is her cousin sister. Then she felt very happy and said she can't live without him and the boy also replied the same they are happy and started working very hard and studying they just concentrate only on studies but they know that that make more closely with their family and they already know that only studies make them together but they are together by heart and fellings not by any other and he was ready to do anything for her but when abiya parents didn't accept their love she decided to die in the sense she want to commit suicide but she tried to attempt suicide but she did n't attempt that because she always remembered how girls are used to facing the evil situation and she doesn't

want to die she wants to
live happily with him.

# Abiya meets her childhood best friends....

One day abiya went to the shopping mall then she found Neha and she was very happy and she and Neha decided to meet all friends next year and they remembered everyone that they had felt very happy .they remembered Raju and varuvan . they thinking how are all. And what they are studying and they felt very sad that they missed them and Abiya and Neha are in contact with each other and other friends are thinking to come back to the village kapiri the next year. All the friends had returned to the village as Raju went to Mumbai he returned to the kapiri to meet friends by train and varuvan returned to kapiri from America by flight and both Neha and Abiya went to kapiri village by bus to meet their friends and Raju reached first to the kapiri village and he started rounding around the village he found this school and old teachers and some other classmates and others and he found the lake and finally went near waterfalls and he was waiting for other friends and Neha and abiya reached the village by afternoon they also went to school and the lake and the next teachers and abiya's old home at kapiri she and Neha  felt very happily . and they reached the lake and Raju waited for them and went to school        he        asked headmaster     permission and sat in the classroom and Neha and abiya are searching for Raju and varuvan and finally both of them meet Raju by evening all those are happy and shared their feelings that Neha is studying architecture and she is going to complete it and settle very happily and all those  friends are waiting for varuvan and the night at the lake they sat and had dinner and sharing  happiness raju said that he went to Mumbai and started a business and he settled ver well and at the night they stayed at the village head house so Neha said that she is going to marry some busssiness ma and raju not of dreamt that and they are ver happy and  waiting for varuvan all the night under the stars and happiness and love they are really happily and Abiya felt this real happiness and at the night raju went for a walk then  he found a car coming . then the car stopped and varuvan get out of car and hugged raju . He got happy tears and both of them surprised Neha and Abiya and them happy and varuvan said he settled in America he became a very successful man. And the next day all the friends went to the lake and enjoyed and also went to waterfalls their they spent a very sweet and memorable moment and they are happy and they got into contact with each other and abiya returned to the city.

# Abiya Meets Kabisha............

Abiya found a girl child on a street road where she is lying on the street road without food and clothes, she looks very thin and lean. Abiya asked her why are you here? where are your parents or the dearest ones of you? she doesn't reply and started crying as she was so lean weak she was unable to speak.so abiya decided to take the girl to her room and she has given some food to eat and clothes. Then later the girl replied that her name is kabisha.

She said that she left by her parents as she was born as a girl. After listening to this abiya started crying later she heard kabisha life. Abiya felt that she had such a great life by her parents. Kabisha said that her parents are very poor they are unable to feed themself and she is the one girl born for them .so they decided to leave her as she was a girl. then abiya realized that many of the girls still now are facing this evil situation from society. And she has known many things like this from kabisha. That many of the girls are left by parents because they were born as girls and some girls used to get married at that little age to an old man and if the man died due to age or some health or other the girl also has died along with him.she realized that why to kill the little girl as her man died and she felt that life is precious and kill the precious girl life is crueler than the killing of the origin. And some are misusing the value of life as their being sold to others that are crueler. The girl is more precious than others because she was not created to be sold for others or the other human use. Even a girl or a woman is also a human.

They have the right to live and had the right to live and equal to men. A girl is not an object to use and through she is the life for the future world. If a girl was not there was this universe could exist. And some girls are misusing it .even now it's not over now you can realize it and stand with courage and walk with divinity.if you are in that situation now start thinking up to get out from that walk with courage be a pride of your self-esteem.if your poor or weak and can't able to do something that you want to achieve in your life just think of that you're born not a worst you are born with the great power and strength. Think of that you are born as a human to achieve big and not be as a looser or some other.

You are lucky to have this life on this wonderful earth .so stand up with the divinity and move as of your real strength. If you are weak of then start thinking to rise not of thinking your situation is worst. And mainly a girl to live in the world with courage. After all, this Abiya decided to change society. later she understood that changing society is not such an easier that thought to fight bigger. She never thinks what the other man thinks of her and she just feels that she know what to be as. And abiya started sending the kabisha to the school for education and by side, she sends kabisha to earn something from what she learns,abiya with her own and supported kabisha that her interests and she promoted it and that makes kabisha to earn. Abiya encouraged her to send to drawing classes where she was very talented and interested in it so she sends to classes and kabisha used to draw beautiful paintings and her talent got recognized by the people she was encouraged for it.And later kabisha shared how her friends are facing problems in village they are treated very bad in their childhood they don't education and some abused and some are sold them to other to export girls for money and sex and they used to marry in very less age and they used to send them to husband's house and that little baby has to face cruel and evil situations from mother-in-law and from husband's family and they can't do any thing they used to remained as helpless and some are used to kill them if they not give high dowry and more money. And they used to look girls in the way of having sex why do don't treat them as your sister or even mother.And always remember create your own identitiy which you are best at and stand up on your own leg so that makes a girl to fight with evil and not to depend on anyone for money or other needs and remember even you are fifty plus also stand up on your own leg not to depend and even after fifity start new things.And fight for the justice and against evil in this society.

# ABIYA UNDERSTOOD THE REALITY OF WOMEN

Abiya understands that the reality of women that a girl was born not to feed up her family and others. If a girl was born was she

136

need to face lot of situations in her life . like while she was child she need to get right education from her parents and good social environment but now in some parts of the world a child girl is used for other uses and she was being torched by others .she need to fight for herself to get this and not only this that is her right to get as human of basic needs and she is being torched from family issues and other issues .she should not left it like that she must fight with power . And stand up with divinity . In ancient days a girl child is respected as a goddess but now what happened .why to use her for physical needs and money use? What happened to the great culture? And many like this.And now present world think in some parts of the world as women for home and other uses like to look up family not only this she has right to earn and has more power to work financially. She just need support and encouragement to do .if it is there she would do many wonder full things .she is the only one who can recrate the world with love so why not to encourage her with love and support .she needs to look up the child and family and house hold chores and she needs to manage her job and not only women but men also look up and take care of financially and family even men face lot of hard situations in life from society and family but even women work financially men always underestimate her . They should know that she can recreate this world. As a tennager she need to take care of her family and manily her studies and financially also some times and she feels she needs free and good social environment . but the reality we see is the she face abusements from this evil situation . she should not backward her step whether her problem is every trouble to family she should stand up with power and walk to get justice for her.

Why to do guys don't understand before doing evil to girl. Why don't you think of it . if the girls is your sibling or some relative would you like to do . why don't you treat her as atleast a women or an human being. This is not the any bluff words it is the reality of the women facing in this society .And some are misusing the womanity and becoming to anti for good society. If you are in such kind of problems just think to rise up. They have to go through many lot of problems like sexual abuse and women harresment and maritial issues and lack of education and many more.support her by educating and stand up with power.

WHERE GIRL IS RESPECTED THERE THEY ARE BLESSED WITH HAPPINESS AND JOY IN LIFE....

Not only that the world remains with peace and

colourful…then abiya decided to stand up with divinity and walk to the throne and make every girl as a great women …

So she decided to start up a team of members who came up to support the girl….she had taken lot of risk fighting with the evil society with the few people .. but she stood up with power and divinity. Can she fight with this society? She startedthink of it ? and she decided to study hard first in that journey she started to know the reality of the girl child more she has gone through many sad and heart touching real life of girls.she decided to fight for every child girl and womens. Let see how she faced lot of problems and know how she became the        more        great women.......

Then she decide to do what we love and that makes happy so she decided to complete her higher education first and wants to enter to wonderful job and mean while she started making herself more strong physically while see is making herself she understands that first every girl should make herself strong by physically and mentally.first that is most important to fight.Andshould ready to face any situation with courage and brave.And also she understood that every human being is not perfect in every part . just they are the perfect in some part of life they develop it as their best .As of now many girls fight for it and many leaders fought for it they achieved the great success and now a little that a women or a girl is walk some golden parts of life is because their strong movements and their power.she started knowing about them and she planning for the right movement and correct plan...........

TOBE CONTINUED.....

LET SEE IN NEXT
SERIES WHETHER
ABIYA GET MARRIED
TO ABHISHEK AND HER
NEXT BEAUTIFUL
FUTURE AND MORE
HARD ,PAINFUL
REALJOURNEY'S
ANDHOW SHE IS GOING
TO FIGHT AND HOW
SHE FACED THE GREAT
PROBLEMS

FROM SOCIETY ………..

STAY TUNED

Thank

you.

152

www.ingramcontent.com/pod-product-compliance
Lightning Source LLC
Chambersburg PA
CBHW021214160726
47994CB00001B/475